A School Trip
To The Fruit Planet

By Maxine Harriton

Illustrated By Kimberly Gardner

Library of Congress Control Number: 2006931439

ISBN 0-9787248-0-1
978-0-9787248-0-1

Printed in China.

In Memory of My Mother
_ M.H.

For my husband, daughter, son in law, and my
wonderful grandkids. Thank you for believing in me.
_ K.G.

Dream High Elementary is on top of the world, far, far away. The kids at Dream High Elementary learn about all kinds of things. They learn about the planets, stars, science, math, and healthy habits. The classes are different, but lots of fun.

Since Dream High Elementary is so far away, everyone has to take a rocmobile to school. A rocmobile is a flying vehicle that has rockets attached to it to give it power.

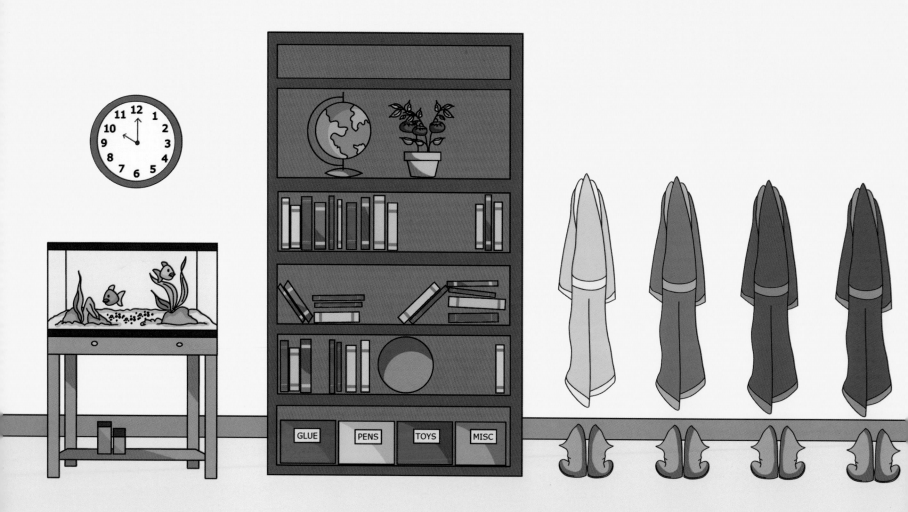

Dawson Reade, Cherry Morgan, and Yin Cato are in Ms. Tillie's class together. They are friends. Ms. Tillie is Dawson's favorite teacher. She always has interesting things under her desk and she takes them on great trips. In her class, Dawson, Cherry, and Yin learn about what kinds of foods to eat to stay healthy.

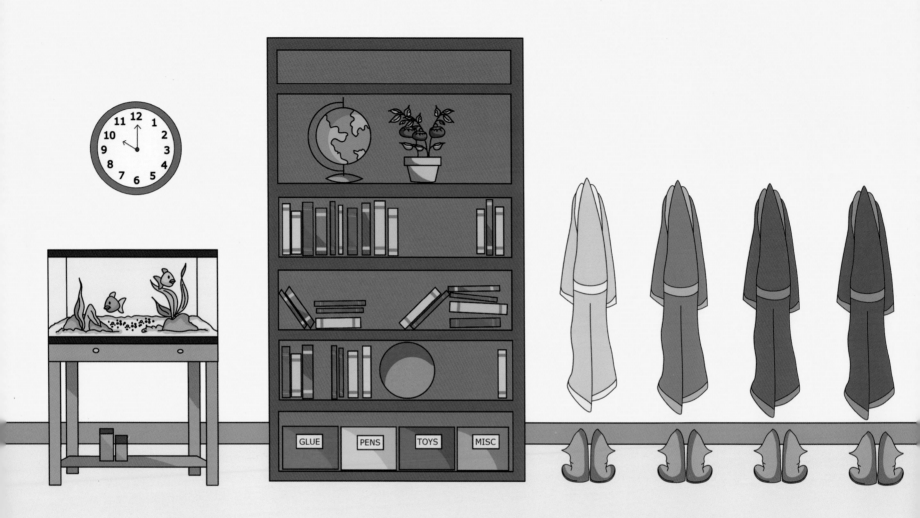

"Eating fruits and vegetables is good for you,"
says Ms. Tillie.

"Draw three of your favorite fruits."

Dawson likes apples, bananas, and grapes.

Cherry likes oranges, pineapple, and pears.

Yin's favorite fruit are cherries, strawberries,
and watermelon.

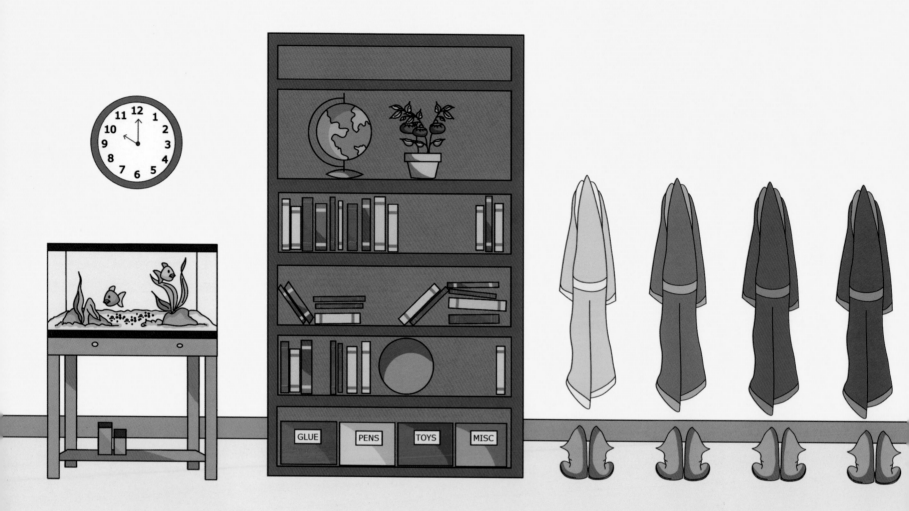

"What kinds of vegetables do you like?" asked Ms. Tillie.

"I don't like vegetables," said Dawson.

"They taste nasty," said Yin.

Ms. Tillie looked at them and shook her head. "You have to eat vegetables to get a healthy body."

"Dawson, what do you want to be when you grow up?" she asked.

"I want to be a captain and travel to other galaxies in the Universe."

"What about you Yin?"

"I want to be an astrophysicist and study how to create stars."
 Ms. Tillie smiled. "Okay,"
"What about you Cherry?"
"I want to be President of the Galaxy."

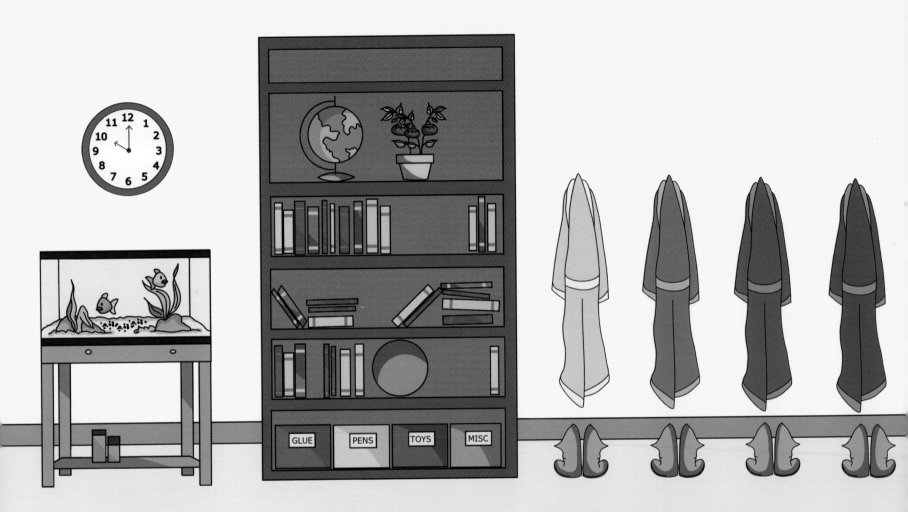

"Well, if you want to do those things, you need to eat fruits and vegetables."

Ms. Tillie took a bag from under her desk. She pulled out a long celery stick. She kept pulling and pulling.

It grew larger, and larger, and longer, and longer. It was so long that it reached to the next planet.

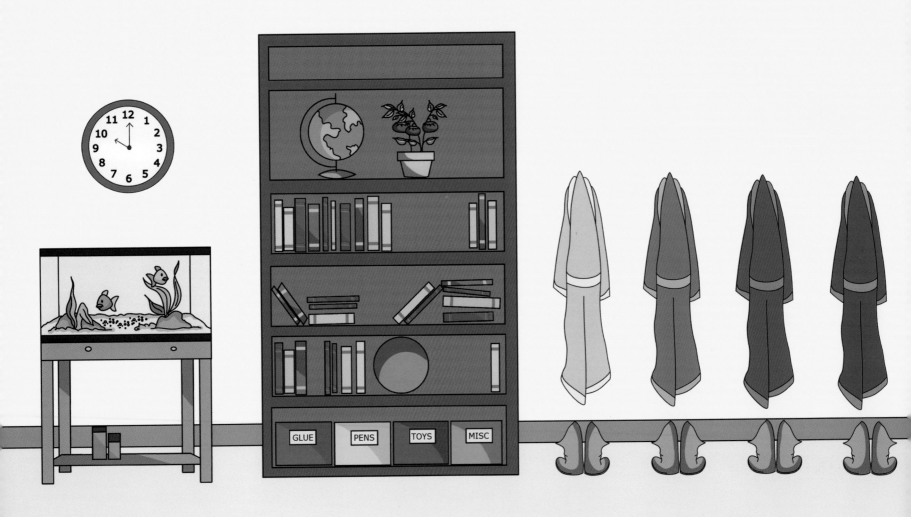

"Ms. Tillie put on her space suit and took another bag from under her desk. The bag was filled with all kinds of fruit."

"C'mon. Let's go," said Ms. Tillie.

"Where are we going?" asked Cherry.

"We're going on a school field trip."

"We may get hungry on the way," said Ms. Tillie.

Riding on Ms. Tillie's rocmobile, with their space suits on, they followed the celery stick.

Midway on the journey, they became hungry. They ate some of the fruit that Ms. Tillie brought.

Dawson had an apple, Cherry an orange, and Yin ate some strawberries.

When they got to the planet, they had to go through a greeting station. The people who greeted them could fly.

Dawson asked Ms. Tillie, "How come these people can fly."

"They eat foods that give them lots of energy," said Ms. Tillie.

After passing through the greeting station, they saw that the planet was filled with all sorts of large looking fruits and vegetables.

Dawson and Yin ran to a giant ear of corn. They climbed the ear of corn. While climbing, they stopped to take a bite out of the corn.

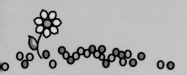

As Cherry watched Dawson and Yin, a cloud of cauliflower appeared over her head. A beam of light came down on her and she started to rise.

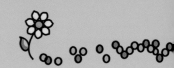

The cauliflower picked everyone up and they all floated through the air. As they floated, they saw all the land. They saw trees that looked like broccoli, grass that looked like green peas, flowers that looked like lemons and oranges, building structures that looked like blueberries, and raspberries.

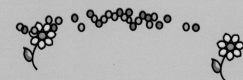

Suddenly, they were dropped into a sea of sea vegetables.

"What is this stuff?" asked Cherry, as she tried to swim.

"It's a mixture of seaweed," said Yin, as he swallowed.

"Look," said Dawson.
"Here comes a boat."
It was a banana boat with lettuce as sails.

They got on the boat. The banana boat took them back to the greeting station.

Before leaving, they had to look at themselves in a mirror. They each looked into the mirror to see how their bodies had changed.

Dawson noticed that he had grown taller. Cherry noticed that her hair grew longer, and Yin felt stronger.

As they headed back to school, they all had so much energy that they were smiling all the way.